A long time ago Chris Owen worked on the Red Funnel Ferry service to the Isle of Wight.

When he spent three years in a tent in the middle of Italy, he dreamt of being a pirate.

He didn't dream of being Hairy Mole exactly, but that's how it turned out.

Chris now lives in sunny Hove, England, right next to the sea. He has written a number of sitcoms and books for grown-ups.

Hairy Mole
the
Pirate

by

Chris Owen

Ransom

Hairy Mole the Pirate

by Chris Owen
Illustrated by David Mostyn

Published by Ransom Publishing Ltd.
Rose Cottage, Howe Hill, Watlington, Oxon. OX49 5HB
www.ransom.co.uk

ISBN   184167 562 8
        978 184167 562 6

First published in 2006

Copyright © 2006 Ransom Publishing Ltd.

Text copyright © 2006 Chris Owen
Illustrations copyright © 2006 David Mostyn

Printed in China through Colorcraft Ltd., Hong Kong.

Thanks to:

All my friends who have put up with me over the years. You know who you are. And thanks to Steve and Jenny for being able to laugh at things that you're not supposed to laugh at and having faith in Hairy Mole.

A big 'thank you' to Nikki Cheal for her support while assisting a technophobe.

Finally, thanks to the Owen family and the Chapman/Persey family, especially Liz Persey, Winnie Randall and Albert Owen, gone but not forgotten.

This book is dedicated to Small & Hubbert (be nice to each other).

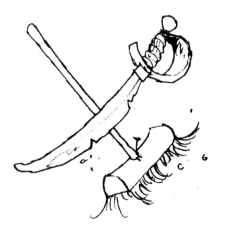

Chris Owen

Chapter One

Hairy Mole the Pirate

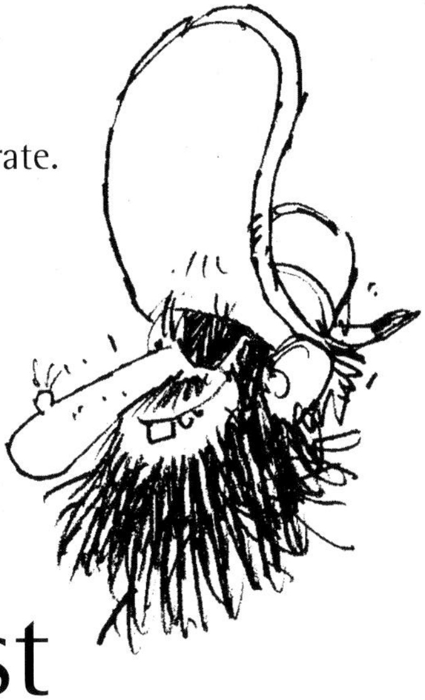

This is a story about Hairy Mole the pirate.

Hairy Mole thought he was the

meanest,

maddest,

roughest,

toughest

pirate that ever lived.

A pirate was all that Hairy Mole had ever wanted to be for as long as he could remember.

His mother, Mrs Bulbous Mole, had encouraged her son whenever she could.

She had fed him:

Extra sugar for black, rotten teeth

Extra turnips for really waxy ears

Extra syrup for greasy hair

And extra sprouts for extra smelly trumps.

Hairy Mole had soon grown into a ferocious pirate.

He had a black bushy beard,

Hideously dirty nails,

A crooked broken nose

And an eye patch over his left eye.

He didn't actually need the eye patch, but he wore it anyway because that's the kind of guy Hairy Mole was – really, really, really, rough!!

Now, like all good – I mean bad – pirates, Hairy Mole had a pirate ship.

Most pirate ships are very large with up to 50 sails and 100 pirates for a crew.

Most pirate ships travel the world to find buried treasure and attack other ships to steal their money and their maps.

9

But Hairy Mole's ship wasn't like most other pirate ships.

Hairy Mole's ship didn't have gold door handles or silver spoons.

Hairy Mole's ship only had two sails and six pirates for crew.

In fact Hairy Mole's little ship hadn't even got as far as the Isle of Wight, let alone travelled around the world.

This didn't stop Hairy Mole from dreaming.

He dreamt of islands where beaches are made of gold dust and the coconuts are giant rubies.

He dreamt of capturing ships and stealing their jam and fine wine.

He even dreamt of selling his pirate stories to the newspapers and becoming as famous as

Blackbeard

who was Hairy Mole's hero (Hairy Mole had posters on his wall and everything).

Chapter Two

Setting Sail

One day Hairy Mole decided enough was enough.

He would follow his dreams and sail his little ship out onto the seven seas in search of adventures and jam.

He told his crew to be ready to leave at 6' o'clock the very next morning.

All the crew were quite shocked that they were actually going anywhere and had got quite used to playing cards and drinking rum without doing any work.

The crew moaned and groaned about why did they have to go anywhere and surely they could just steal some jam from Mrs Plop's jam shop. But Hairy Mole was having none of it and ordered them to their hammocks for a good sleep before the next day's adventure.

Now the crew moaned and groaned even louder because they didn't like going to bed early. Hairy Mole was still not having a bean of it and shouted:

"If you don't all go to your hammocks right now, I'll cut off your ears and have them in ear sandwiches!"

There were no more moans and groans after that. Well there were, but Hairy Mole didn't hear them. He went to his own hammock and listened to the creaking of his ship and the

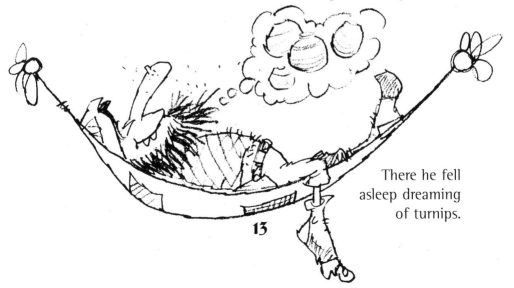

There he fell asleep dreaming of turnips.

13

The next morning at 6' o'clock on the dot, Hairy Mole let out a loud

y a w n

and leapt from his hammock. The sun was just poking through one of the ship's round windows and Hairy Mole smiled to himself as he got dressed.

Hairy Mole put on his special pirate costume that had been washed and ironed by his mother, Mrs Mole. The clothes still smelled like lemons from the washing powder and Hairy Mole raised his big bushy eyebrows as he thought of what Blackbeard would make of a pirate smelling like lemons!

There he stood: shirt, boots, belt, pirate hat and pantaloons.

He was ready for anything.

He quietly tip-toed up the wooden steps onto the little wooden deck and stared at the sea before him.

A seagull squawked as it flew by.

"Nice day for being a pirate," the bird, who was called Toby, cried out.

"Even nicer to be a seagull," Hairy Mole replied.

With that Toby flew high into the air and Hairy Mole watched him until he was out of sight. Now the only sounds came from below deck as the crew continued to snore and parp in their morning snoozing.

Hairy Mole shook his head as he listened to an extra loud parp.

"This will never do," he grumbled and with that he strode over to the ship's mast.

On the mast was a hook and from the hook there was a bell and from the bell there was a rope and this was the rope that Hairy Mole now held in his hairy hand as he rang the bell for all he was worth.

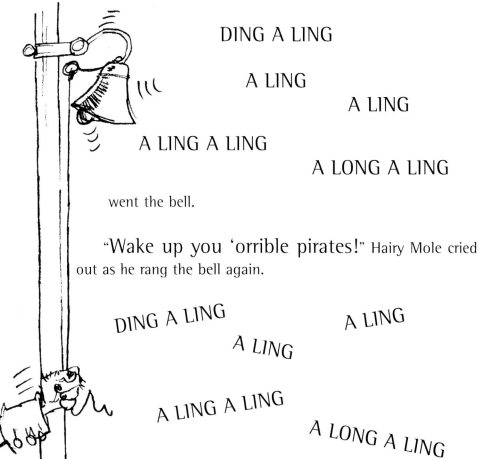

DING A LING

A LING

A LING

A LING A LING

A LONG A LING

went the bell.

"Wake up you 'orrible pirates!" Hairy Mole cried out as he rang the bell again.

DING A LING   A LING

A LING

A LING A LING

A LONG A LING

went the bell again.

Slowly, one by one, the pirates woke up and joined Hairy Mole on deck. They blinked and rubbed their eyes as they stood in the morning sunshine scratching their pits and fastening their pantaloons.

"Right, name check," bellowed Hairy Mole as he stood before them, his buttons shining and his bristles twitching.

"Belch?"

"Here," said Belch.

"Pickle?"

"Here," said Pickle.

"Crevice & Pit, the twins?"

"Here, there," said Crevice 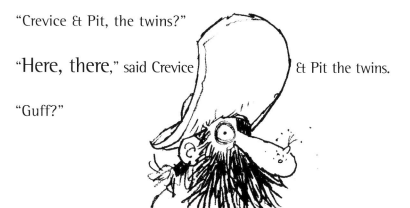 & Pit the twins.

"Guff?"

There was silence.

17

"Guuuuuuf?" Hairy Mole bellowed. The other

4 pirates turned to where Guff was supposed to be standing. She was nowhere to be seen.

"Perhaps she has fallen overboard," suggested Pickle.

"Perhaps she's been eaten by seagulls," suggested Belch.

"Perhaps she has run away to become an insurance salesman," suggested Crevice & Pit together.

"Perhaps she is a lazy toad and hasn't got her lazy bag of bones out of bed yet!" cried Hairy Mole and rang the bell extra loudly so not only Guff could hear but half the town as well.

"All right, all right." Guff yawned as she crawled up the wooden steps, and out onto the wooden deck, scratching her ribs and picking her nose.

There they stood, in line, shuffling from foot to foot as Hairy Mole inspected them.

Belch was the tallest and had the biggest nose.

Pickle was second tallest and had the biggest feet.

Crevice & Pit, being twins, were exactly the same size yet they both had the biggest hands.

Which just leaves one   tiny   Guff who had the biggest ears.

Chapter Three

Mr Bogey

As Hairy Mole stood shaking his head at the rabble before him a strange sound was heard coming up the gangplank.

STAMP, KNOCK

STAMP, KNOCK

STAMP, KNOCK

STAMP, KNOCK

"What's that noise?" cried Guff, as she had the biggest ears.

STAMP, KNOCK

STAMP, KNOCK

STAMP, KNOCK

"Ah ha!" whooped Hairy Mole. "That will be my surprise!"

And with that they all ran to the edge of the ship and looked over the side and down the gangplank.

On the gangplank stood the scariest pirate that any of the crew had ever seen.

He had long black hair and a big black hat with a feather sticking out of it. A big bushy beard and a crooked nose; a big fat belly from too much rum; and finally the most gruesome sight of all, at the end of his left leg there was a cricket bat.

There the pirate stood, on the gangplank, staring at the crew. There the crew stood, on the boat, staring at the pirate.

"Ah ha!" the pirate shouted and continued walking up the plank until he was on deck.

STAMP, KNOCK

STAMP, KNOCK

"This is my first mate, Mr Bogey." Hairy Mole shook hands with Mr Bogey and Mr Bogey shook hands with Hairy Mole.

"Green will be my first mate on our voyage across the seven seas. You shall call him Mr Bogey and only Mr Bogey. When I am asleep he will be in charge, when I am eating he will be the captain and if I am attacked by giant seagulls

who carry me off to their nest then Mr Bogey will continue as captain of my ship. Now does everyone understand?"

There was more shuffling of feet and nodding of heads as Hairy Mole looked along the crew.

"Do you have anything to add, Green old mate?" Hairy Mole turned to his one legged friend.

Mr Bogey puffed out his barrel-shaped chest and bristled his eyebrows like a cat arching its back. Then he rose on his one good foot and started to speak.

"Thank you Hairy Mole," squeaked Mr Bogey. Because although he was very **fierce** and **gruesome** looking, he had an extremely high-pitched and incredibly squeaky voice.

"I would just like to add," Mr Bogey squeaked a squeaky little cough.

"I like my eggs to be runny in the morning, soft at lunchtime and hard for my supper. Any questions?"

Mr Bogey looked at the crew before him. One eyebrow rose as he crossed his arms and waited.

Belch shuffled his feet.

Pickle scratched his head.

And Crevice and Pit shook their heads at the same time.

"I have a question!" piped up Guff.

"Go ahead," squeaked Mr Bogey.

"Why have you got a **cricket bat** for a leg?"

Everyone stood in stunned silence as Mr Bogey turned his attention to Guff.

Everyone watched as Mr Bogey s l o w l y walked over to where Guff was standing.

STAMP KNOCK
STAMP KNOCK

Guff began to tremble, as Mr Bogey stood right in front of her.

Guff looked up at Mr Bogey's hairy nostrils and began to realise just how Mr Green Bogey got his name.

"Never!" Mr Bogey squeaked.

"Never!" He squeaked again.

"Never sail to the West Indies when it's raining!"

With that Mr Bogey turned around and quickly stomped back over to Hairy Mole.

24

STAMP KNOCK

"Right, enough talking!" shouted Hairy Mole.

"Let's find treasure and jam."

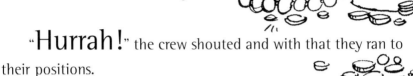

"Hurrah!" the crew shouted and with that they ran to their positions.

Mr Bogey squealed out orders to the crew.

"Hoist the main sail, pull up the anchor, scrub the decks and Yo ho ho where's my rum!"

Belch and Pickle undid the two sails until they bulged in the wind.

Crevice and Pit pulled in the anchor and undid the ropes until the ship finally started to move away from the dock.

They sailed out of the harbour and waved to the other boats until they were out of sight. They sailed out onto the open seas, until all that they could see was sea.

Chapter Four

Out on the Ocean

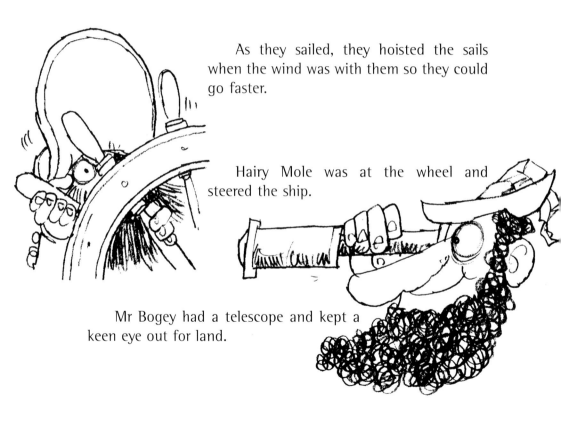

As they sailed, they hoisted the sails when the wind was with them so they could go faster.

Hairy Mole was at the wheel and steered the ship.

Mr Bogey had a telescope and kept a keen eye out for land.

The sea got *rougher* as the winds began to blow.

The waves got *bigger* as the winds blew stronger.

Everyone held onto the sides of the ship as it went

up and down

up and down

and then

side to side

and up and down again.

The little ship was tossed about all over the place and it began to creak and squeak as the waves battered its little sides.

Crevice and Pit huddled in a corner as the mighty waves crashed over the sides.

Guff felt a little bit sick and turned a strange shade of green.

Pickle, who was down below trying to cook supper, was battered about all over the place. Pots and pans came crashing down as he tried to catch fish fingers as they flew over his head.

Belch and Guff got big buckets and tipped the water over the sides of the ship as the water splashed on to the deck.

Hairy Mole and Mr Bogey wrestled with the wheel as the ship went up and down and side to side . Mr Bogey held onto his hat with the feather in the top, just as hard as he held onto the wheel. He /ʌved that hat!

Everyone was

s
o
a
k
i
n

g   wet as they held their positions and waited for the winds to stop blowing.

After a couple of hours the winds died down. Pickle had finally managed to catch the fish fingers and everyone dried themselves ready for tea. Even Guff was feeling a little bit peckish and had returned to her normal shade of pink.

As they sat around the table and were just about to take their first bite of finger, a loud squeak came from out on deck.

"EEEEEEEEEEEEEEEEK!" went the squeak, so perhaps it should have been a loud eek - but it doesn't really matter. Everyone looked up at the little door leading to the deck.

"LAND, LAND, LAND I see land ahoy!"

With that, everyone put down their pirate knives and forks and pushed their way onto the deck.

There, in the distance, was an island.

Chapter Five

Land Ahoy!

As the island got closer, the crew watched the seagulls flying overhead. One looked exactly like Toby the Seagull from the port, but then again all seagulls look the same.

The island sand shimmered in the sunlight.

Guff put one hand to her oversized left ear and listened.

"I hear drums!" Guff declared.

"OOOOOOᴼᴼᴼooooo!" ooooooooed the others, all together.

Slowly, Hairy Mole steered the ship towards the island, and the closer they got the bigger it became.

Crevice and Pit jumped up and down with excitement.

"Will there be treasure, will there be treasure?" they both squealed excitedly.

Guff rubbed her belly and licked her lips "Will there be jam?" She raised her eyebrows as they all turned to Hairy Mole.

Hairy Mole s l o w l y took off his big pirate hat

and s l o w l y rubbed his big pirate beard.

Then he s l o w l y started to smile, a broad, beaming smile that showed every one of his blackened teeth.

"There will be enough **treasure** and **jam** for us all to enjoy," he shouted.

"Hurrah!" went the crew.

"What about eggs?" asked Mr Bogey.

"Hhhhmmm! Probably," answered Hairy Mole with an extremely raised eyebrow.

As the little ship got closer to the shore, the golden sand and the green of the palm trees could clearly be seen.

The water was a crystal blue and amazingly coloured fish could be seen beneath the surface.

As the ship got closer, still the sound of drums began to grow louder.

BOOM,

BOOM,

BOOMTITTY BOOM went the drums.

Filled with the excitement of treasure and jam, the pirates j u m p e d from the boat into the s h a l l o w water surrounding the island.

"Where's the treasure, Hairy Mole, where's the treasure?" sang Crevice and Pit together.

"Jam, jam, we want some jam," sang along Guff.

"I hope there are lots of lovely r u n n n y eggs," thought Mr Bogey to himself.

The pirates ran onto the beach and busied themselves digging in the sand.

Guff made a nice sandcastle with turrets and a moat.

This wasn't exactly what Hairy Mole had in mind, so he knocked it over and shouted: "You're supposed to be digging, not building!" Hairy Mole was s e c r e t l y impressed by Guff's castle but didn't tell her because he was a pirate and pirates just don't do that sort of thing.

Suddenly, from out of the palm trees came a Nudey Man. All he was wearing was a band around his head and a necklace around his neck.

All the pirates stopped digging and stared, which is usually quite rude but also quite acceptable in these sorts of circumstances.

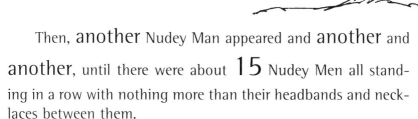

Then, another Nudey Man appeared and another and another, until there were about 15 Nudey Men all standing in a row with nothing more than their headbands and necklaces between them.

Hairy Mole stood up and counted the Nudey Men:

1, 2, 3, 4, 5, 6, 7, 8, 9, 10, 11, 12, 13, 14, 15.

15 Nudey Men.

Then Mr Bogey nudged him in the chest.

"Look at their necklaces!" squeaked Mr Bogey.

Hairy Mole looked at the necklaces.

Now these necklaces weren't the usual type with shells and beads. These necklaces were made of fingers and noses, ears and toes, and not forgetting knees and elbows!

"Eeek!" said Hairy Mole.

Suddenly a giant, fat Nudey Man appeared behind the others. And do you know what he was carrying?

Here's a clue, was it:

a) – a box of chocolates?

b) – a bunch of flowers?

Or was it C – a cooking pot ???

Put it this way: the pirates turned and ran back to their ship as quickly as they could. Even Mr Bogey ran and he had a **cricket bat** for a leg!

The **Nudey Men** started to dance around the bunch of flowers, I mean cooking pot, and shouted to the pirates.

"Run away!" shouted Hairy Mole.

"Run away, they'll eat us all!"

The pirates got onto their ship and left the island at record-breaking speed.

Up went the sails, up went the anchor and off went the pirates, all breathing a **big sigh** of relief.

Back on the island the Nudey Men sat down around the cooking pot.

"Maybe they don't like my potato and leek soup," said the fat Nudey Man to Nudey Man number 15.

"Obviously not vegetarians. Anyway there's no pleasing pirates!" shrugged Nudey Man 15.

But it was too late, as the little pirate ship continued on its voyage in search of treasure and jam.

Chapter Six

Sea, Sea and more Sea!

After the pirates had recovered from almost getting eaten they headed south.

The sun was h^{o}t and they all lazed on deck working on their sun tans and licking frozen fish fingers, which was the closest that they could get to ice creams.

Hairy Mole sat down below, itching his beard and scratching his noggin. He thought of the adventure on the island and smiled. "No treasure but a good story to tell," he thought to himself.

Shortly, Mr Bogey came down below to sit with Hairy Mole.

Stamp knock.
Stamp knock.

Hairy Mole looked up from his thoughts.

"Yo ho ho Hairy Mole," squeaked Mr Bogey.

"Yo ho ho Mr Bogey," replied Hairy Mole.

They sat together in silence listening to the sounds of the seagulls and the lapping of the waves against the sides of the little ship.

The heat of the day and the movement of the ship slowly made Hairy Mole feel sleepy and it was not long before he was snoring in time with the movement of the ship.

Honk phew
Honk phew
Honk pheeeew

snored Hairy Mole.

Mr Bogey also drifted into sleep, resting his hat with the feather in the top over his face.

Eeek squeak
Eeek squeak
Eeek squeeeeeak

snored Mr Bogey.

Chapter Seven

A Strange Ship Ahoy!

As the day drew on, the crew lazed on deck. They paddled their pirate toes in the cool refreshing water, they watched the flying fish flying out of the sea and Guff idly put her hand out to try and catch one.

Crevice and Pit sat back-to-back reading comics, while Belch lay in his hammock squinting at the sunshine. Pickle had taken it upon himself to stand by the wheel and pretend he knew what he was doing.

"Left a bit Pickle," shouted Guff playfully.

"No, right a bit," called out Belch.

They all laughed as Pickle ignored them and looked out to sea.

"Look out for that **giant** ship," laughed out Crevice.

"Yes, look out for that **giant** ship... Oh my goodness! GIANT SHIP, GIANT SHIP AHOY," Guff shouted excitedly.

Everyone ran to the side of the deck and s t a r e d at the **giant** ship.

The ship was **huge**. With up to 20 sails and at least 4 masts it bobbed on the water, not moving anywhere. Slowly, Pickle steered the little ship and wished he had never pretended he actually knew how to steer in the first place.

"What's all this? What's all this?" Hairy Mole stuck his hairy head out from down below and stepped onto the deck.

"Stop that steering Pickle and way Hey the anchor Crevice and Pit. Action stations everybody."

With that Hairy Mole's little ship stopped moving and began to bob up and down in front of the giant ship before them.

The crew stared at the ship. They were now so close that they could hear the creaking of the vessel in front of them.

"There's no crew aboard! Where are the crew?" Mr Bogey squeaked.

"Perhaps they are all asleep," suggested Guff.

"Perhaps they have gone swimming," suggested Crevice and Pit together.

"Perhaps this ship is empty and we can climb on board and have it for ourselves," cried out Pickle.

"Hurrah hurrah hurrah hurrah hurrah!" everyone shouted at the same time.

"Right, set up the ropes, let us board that ship and eat their jam!" Hairy Mole shouted excitedly.

"We may not have found a treasure island but at least we have found a treasure ship!"

"Hurrah, hurrah!" cried the pirates together, again.

With that they grabbed ropes and tied them to the mast. They quickly swung across the sea and onto the giant ship.

"Wheeeeyheeeey!" they squealed as they landed on the other ship's deck.

The giant ship was d e s e r t e d . No-one could be seen anywhere. Quietly Hairy Mole ordered them all to split up and search the ship to see if they could find anyone - or more importantly any treasure.

Pickle and Belch went to the left.

Crevice and Pit went to the right.

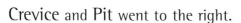

Hairy Mole and Guff went down below.

While Mr Bogey volunteered to stay right where he was, just in case something

happened.

Pickle and Belch returned after finding no-one on the left.

Crevice and Pit returned after finding no-one on the right.

Hairy Mole and Guff returned after finding no-one down below.

And Mr Bogey.

Mr Bogey was nowhere to be seen.

"Where's Mr Bogey?" asked Guff in a quiet voice.

"He's probably gone back to our little ship!" said Hairy Mole in a gruff voice.

"He might have fallen in," suggested Crevice and Pit together.

"He could have found some treasure," whispered Pickle.

"Why are you whispering," asked Belch.

"So the ghost pirates that have captured Mr Bogey don't hear me!" whispered Pickle.

"Oh!" they all said together.

"OOOOOOOOOOOHHHHHHH!!!!!"

they all said again, but this time a lot more loudly.

The crew all looked at Mr Bogey, as he stood tied to the mast. His hair had turned white underneath his hat with the feather in the top, and his good knee knocked against his cricket bat leg as the ghost pirates surrounded him.

"Eeeeek!" squeaked Mr Bogey.

"Yikes!" replied the crew.

"OOOOOOOOOOOOOOOOOOOOOOOOOOOOOOOOOOOOOHHHHH!" called the ghost pirates as they noticed the rest of the crew.

The ghost pirates floated towards Hairy Mole.

"OOOOOOOOOOOOOOOHHHHHH!"

went the ghost pirates again.

"Follow me!" Hairy Mole cried and started to run along the ship.

Pickle ran after Hairy Mole.

Belch ran after Pickle.

Crevice and Pit ran after Belch.

Guff ran after the twins.

And the ghost pirates floated after Guff.

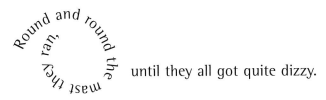 until they all got quite dizzy.

Hairy Mole grabbed hold of the piece of rope that tied up Mr Bogey, and as they ran the rope untied, so Mr Bogey joined in the running too.

"Abandon ghost ship!" shouted Hairy Mole. All the crew   jumped   off
                          the
                             ghost ship
                                    and
                                        onto their own little ship.
They were so scared they didn't even need ropes.

"Way Hey anchor!" shouted Hairy Mole.

" Hoist the sails! " squeaked Mr Bogey.

With everyone on board, the little ship sailed off as quickly as it could, leaving the ghost pirates f l$_0$ at $_i$ n g on the side of their giant ghost ship.

"Well, that was nice wasn't it!" said one ghost pirate to the next.

"There we were, practising our knots, when that chap with the cricket bat got all tied up!"

"I know!" said the next ghost pirate.

"All I was going to say was OOOOOOOOOHHHHHH what a lovely little ship, but they never gave me the chance!"

With that the ghost pirates watched as the little ship sailed out of sight. Then they returned to their tea of banana sandwiches and spicy tomatoes.

"That was close!" squeaked Mr Bogey as everyone calmed down and the giant ship disappeared out of sight.

"Very close indeed," replied Hairy Mole.

Chapter Eight

A Spot of Fishing

The little ship continued to sail through the night and into the next day, without seeing another thing except for sea, sea and more sea. The crew went about their chores cleaning decks and knotting rope, drinking rum and playing cards.

But soon the pirates grew tired and weary. All they had to eat were fish fingers, and it wasn't long before they were all dreaming of roast dinners and barbecues.

"I'm bored of fish fingers," declared Guff, "I want to eat a whole fish, not just its fingers!"

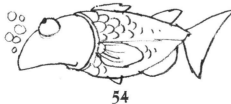

"Us too, no more f^{i}s$_h$ f$_i$ng^{er}s," shouted out the twins together.

"Well how do you all propose that we catch some fish?" asked Hairy Mole with one raised bushy eyebrow.

"With this!" called out Pickle.

They all turned to look at Pickle as he stood holding on to the mast.

In his hand Pickle was holding a rope, and at the end of the rope was a frozen f^{i}s$_h$ f$_i$ng^{er}.

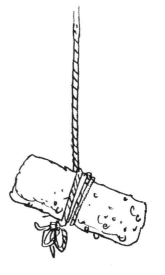

"All
    we have

        to   do

          is

hold the f^{i}s$_h$ f$_i$ng^{er} in the water and when the fish see it they will be so curious as to where the rest of the fish is they will jump out of the water, onto the deck, and ask us what is going on." Pickle b e a m e d from ear to ear at the genius of his plan.

55

"Fantastic plan Pickle, but perhaps we should just use this net instead?" Belch produced the fishing net from down below and everyone gathered round to decide who was going to start fishing first.

Pickle sat on his own, cross-legged, looking out to sea, while everyone drew straws to see who would use the net.

"Curiosity caught the fish, surely they must understand," thought Pickle to himself.

Finally it was decided that Belch would start the fishing first. He sat with the net in the water and it wasn't long before the net was bulging with fish of all different sizes and colours.

The fish were put into a large pot and it wasn't long before the pot was overflowing.

" I think we have got enough fish now, Belch, " Hairy Mole called out as he looked at the bulging pOt.

"Just one more, Hairy Mole, just one more," called back Belch, who was well into the swing of things.

"OK, just one, but **fish** don't grow on **trees** you know!" replied Hairy Mole, chuckling to himself at Belch's enthusiasm.

"WoooooooooooooooooooooooooooooMama!"

"Just one, Belch," chuckled Hairy Mole again as he heard Belch's enthusiastic shout.

"ooooooooooooooooooohhhhMygosh!"

"Yes, yes, well done." Hairy Mole shook his head, laughing at the expressions of youth.

As Hairy Mole stood shaking his head chuckling to himself, the sky suddenly turned black.

The birds stopped squawking

and the winds stopped blowing.

Hairy Mole shivered, as the world without the sun is a very cold place.

Slowly he turned round to face Belch and the rest of the crew, and there before him was

the
most
gigantic,

enormous, massive,

huge,
gigantic

(that's how big it was - it was double gigantic)

fish

that Hairy Mole had ever seen.

The giant fish was, in fact, a whale and the whale opened his mouth so that the pirate crew could see the whale's gigantic whale tongue, the whale's gigantic whale teeth, the whale's gigantic whale tonsils and finally waggling at the back of the whale's throat like two huge church bells was the whale's gigantic whale epiglottis!

"AAAAAArrrrrgggghhhh!!" screamed all the pirates.

"AAAAAAAAAAhhhhhhh" yawned the whale as he swallowed the pirate ship, the pirate crew and the pirate fishing net all in one go.

The sea was silent apart from the occasional squawking seagull overhead. The patch of water where the little ship had been was still, apart from the occasional b$_u$^{bb}le and ripple of the waves.

Deep, deep, deep under the ocean the whale swam until finally he rested on the ocean floor. The whale closed his tiny whale eyes and went to sleep.

Now deep inside the whale's tummy was a little ship and on that little ship there was Hairy Mole and his pirate crew.

There was Pickle, Belch, Crevice and Pit, Mr Bogey, Guff and finally Hairy Mole.

The whale's tummy was dark and the only way the pirates could see was by the glow of the fish fingers

(that must have had far too much food colouring to be good for anything apart from lighting up a sleeping whale's tummy).

"Well, how are we going to get out of this one?" Hairy Mole turned to the rest of the crew who could be seen in the soft orange light.

"We could ask the whale nicely," suggested Crevice and Pit, the twins.

Hairy Mole raised his eyebrows to the full extent of their raising capacity.

"We could wait until the whale has had its fill of food and sneak out the back door when nature does its business," suggested Pickle, much to everyone's disgust. With that Pickle went and sat, cross-legged, on his own and stared at the sides of the whale's rib cage.

"I never wanted to be a pirate anyway," thought Pickle. "I always wanted to be a thinker and just sit and think about things."

"SSSSSShhhhhh Pickle, I'm thinking," said Hairy Mole, much to Pickle's surprise.

Hairy Mole scratched his big chin and pondered.

He pondered several options, apart from Pickle's, until he couldn't ponder anymore.

"Aaaaatisssho o o o o ! ! o o ! ! " sneezed Guff all of a sudden.

"SSSSSShhhhhh, Guff, I'm pondering," said Hairy Mole as he continued to pace up and down.

"It's not my fault, it's Mr Bogey's hat with the feather in it. The feather makes me sneeze!" said Guff, before sneezing again.

"Aaaaaatisssshhhh o o o ! ! " o o ! o o o ! !

"Sorry," said Mr Bogey taking off his favourite hat with the feather in it.

"I've got it!!" cried Pickle.

Everyone turned to Pickle as he leapt to his feet with his arms in the air.

"What have you got?" asked Hairy Mole.

"Is it catching?" asked Crevice and Pit huddling together.

"An idea, I have an idea!"

With that, Pickle le^ap^t over to Mr Bogey and grabbed the hat from his hands. Then he jumped up onto the mast and

started to climb up the po l e.

"My hat!" squeaked Mr Bogey. "Where is the rascal going with my hat?"

But it was too late. Pickle was up to the top of the mast before you could say "Don't talk to me about climbing up masts inside of whales with a hat that makes you sneeze."

"Genius!" Hairy Mole shouted as he realised what Pickle was doing.

The rest of the crew looked on in wonder, as Pickle started to tickle the side of the whale's rib cage with the feather from Mr Bogey's hat.

He tickled him

to the left   and then the right,

then the top

and then the bottom.

63

Slowly, the whale awoke and felt sort of strange. Slowly the whale started to *smile* as the corners of his lips turned up.

Then the whale started to grin as he showed his **gigantic** teeth.

Then the whale started to s^{h}a k e as his ribs were tickled, and before you know it the whale (whose name was Simon) started to laugh out loud and cry with the tickling sensation that was tickling his ribs.

"Stop it, stop it **please**," cried Simon.

Then Simon started to feel a twitching in his nose. Then Simon started to feel an itching and a twitching, then more itching and more twitching until suddenly...

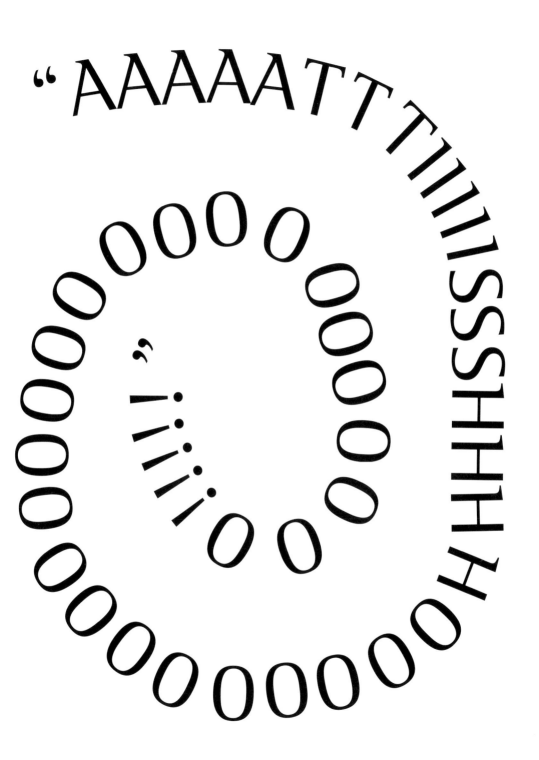

The little pirate ship shot out of Simon the whale's mouth quicker than a slippery piglet in a tree.

The ship whiZZed through the water until it burst onto the sea with an almighty SSSSPLOOOOOOSSSSSHHH!

The crew hung on for dear life as the ship flew through the air. The force of the sneeze blew the little sails inside out until finally the little pirate ship fell onto the ocean with a terrific

PPPLLLOOOOOPPPP P P P P P !!

All the crew stood up and wiped themselves down. Unfortunately none of them had handkerchiefs because they were pirates and didn't really think they would need them, so there they stood all covered in Simon's sn_ot. But they were happy just to be alive.

"That was a lucky escape, Hairy Mole," a voice squawked from above. Hairy Mole looked up to see a friendly face.

"Yes it was, Toby. Perhaps it wasn't such a good day to be a pirate after all!" said Hairy Mole.

"Well you never know unless you try!" squawked Toby the seagull, and with that he turned and flew into the wind, doing somersaults as he went.

Chapter Nine

Out of the Frying Pan

Simon Whale itched himself with his tail. His irritated nose was still slightly tickling somewhat and he was very pleased to have got rid of the unpleasant sensation in his rib cage. He didn't usually like sneezing at the best of times but he especially didn't like it when it involved shooting pirates out of his nostrils.

Simon Whale blinked as a drop of rain fell from the sky and landed on his face. "Looks like rain," he said to no one in particular, before submerging beneath the ocean surface.

As Simon dived, his huge weight forced the water to swell and rise, causing Hairy Mole's little ship to soar high

into the air on the crest of a gianormous wave.

Higher and higher they flew, up into the black storm clouds and up into the rain above, before they were suddenly plunged back down,
down,
down to the ocean below.

All the crew were slipping and sliding from one side of the deck to the other. Desperately they clung onto whatever they could.

Pickle, still holding Mr Bogey's feathered hat, held on tightly to the rigging, wrapping his large feet around the old creaking rope.

The twins, Crevice and Pit, had taken refuge down below and they both curled up tight in the sleeping quarters as the gigantic waves swept the little boat high, high, high into the air before dropping her low, low, low again.

Mr Bogey and Belch held on to the mast as the waves and rain crashed against the deck, swashing masses of green, whale snot down into the galley below.

Guff found herself swept along the deck as the little ship tilted high into the air. She began to slide faster and faster in the b$_u$^{b}bl$_i$n^g water until she could hold on no longer.

Guff was heading straight for the edge when out of nowhere a hairy, warty hand with black fingernails grabbed her by the pigtails. "Arrrrrgggghhhh!!!" she screamed in both surprise and pain.

"Come on Guff, we're not finished yet!" Hairy Mole had managed to strap himself onto the ship's wheel with his 'Made to Last' genuine, pirate belt. Undoing the final notch he stretched the belt over Guff until they were both securely fastened to the wheel.

There they all stood. Gripping, holding, clasping and hanging on for their dear lives. The wind and the rain of the storm continued long into the night and there were many occasions where the rigging strained to breaking and the mast creaked as if it was going to crack. The galley was almost full and sinking and Hairy Mole's 'Made to Last' genuine pirate belt looked like it had seen its last hairy pirate belly button.

"How do we get out of this one?"

thought Hairy to himself, his face stinging from the salty ocean waves and his eyes hurting from the blistering stormy winds.

All everybody could do was just hang on in the darkness.

71

Chapter Ten

'Where's Belch?'

The crew were weak and battered as the first signs of morning crept onto the little ship's deck. They hadn't managed to sleep, except for Belch who had caught 40 winks or so, standing up like a horse.

Through the night the waves had become less and less high, high, high and more and more low, low, low.

And as the bright sunshine chased away the dark storm clouds, the crew fell onto the broken deck bruised and hungry but thankful to be alive.

Hairy Mole released himself and Guff from his 'Made to Last' pirate belt. As he undid the buckle from the stretched and strained leather, the belt disintegrated in his hands.

"They don't make them like they used to!" Hairy Mole smiled and wiped his brow with his wet sleeve. He looked around the little ship. Most of the crew lay exhausted and tired on the deck; the sails were ripped and torn and the deck was cracked and full of holes. The sun began to beat down on the pirates as they bobbed up and down, up and down on the calming ocean waters.

Crevice and Pit appeared from where they had been sheltering down below. They were clutching their bellies and shaking their heads. "Hairy Mole, everybody, we are alive, but we are also ever so, ever so hungry!"

"We're all hungry boys. I would say that that was the worst storm I have ever encountered. Goodness knows how we all survived."

Hairy Mole looked on as his hungry, exhausted crew lay battered and tired on the deck, nodding their heads and holding their empty bellies.

"I would venture that that storm was worse than the great storm of '46!" squeaked Mr Bogey rubbing his stubbly chin. All the pirates nodded thoughtfully and scratched their chins in agreement.

"I would even go as far as to say that it was worse than the terrific storm of '64!" Mr Bogey squeaked again, eyeing the crew with a beady eye.

'Paaaaaarp!!' trumped Belch with an almost musical sound. "Sorry!"

"I'm hungry," he added.

"Now, I reckon that bottom burp was worse than all those storms put together!" laughed Pickle. They all laughed and hugged each other in the bright sunshine and for a moment they forgot their hungry stomachs and their weary limbs. Belch plodded off to the galley with a guilty smile on his face as the rest of the crew sat down nursing their sore arms and their tired heads.

"OK crew, we need to fix this little ship, there is much to be done." Hairy Mole looked at his crew as they lay before him. He knew that they couldn't work without food but he also knew that they couldn't sail without work. Slowly the men got to their feet or crawled over to the nearest hole or the nearest breakage.

Hairy Mole was proud of his friends as they tried their best to mend the broken ship. But it was a never-ending task, as the more they mended the more leaks appeared.

They worked hard through the hot morning sun and all that could be heard was the occasional bang, bang, bang of a hammer or the more than occasional grumble, rumble, tumble of an empty tummy.

After a couple of hours' work Hairy Mole was thinking to himself that saving the little ship would be an impossible task, when suddenly . . .

'Ding a ling a ling!'

The pirates couldn't believe their mouldy ears. Was that the dinner bell???? Why was the dinner bell ringing????

"That's one joke too far from that blithering Belch." Pickle rolled onto his elbow and squinted towards the galley.

'Ding a ling a ling a liiiiing!' The bell sounded again, this time accompanied by a "Grub's up!"

Now all the pirates' attention was firmly centred on the galley. Their tired minds willed Belch to appear with a giant chicken or a huge chunk of cheese. "Does he have eggs, does he have eggs?" whimpered Mr Bogey quietly to himself.

Then, bathed in a golden light, Belch appeared from the galley steps clutching a gigantic, black stewpot inbetween both his warty hands. The pirates' nostrils quivered, the pirates' nostrils sniffed and finally the pirates' nostrils shook as the huge cauldron was slammed down upon the creaking wooden deck.

The bubbling, green stew slopped over the sides and clung to the outside of the pot. Each of the pirates watched silently as a trickle plopped on to the deck and lay bubbling before them.

"Stew for all, me hearties!" cried Belch, laughing, as his friends eagerly grabbed the little wooden bowls and the little wooden spoons that he had hanging out of his pockets. The pirates began to pour the green stew into the bowls and then down their ravenous gullets.

"What? Where? How? Belch?" The questions came inbetween mouthfuls and sometimes straight out of full mouths and sounded more like: "Whap? Wherf? Howf? Belth?" But he still understood.

"Urrrm . . . it's from the cupboard that doesn't get used that often. Urrrm, towards the back, yes, towards the back."

"Who cares!" cried Guff filling up her third bowl of Belch's special, salty, sea broth. "Three cheers for Belch!".

"Hup Hup Horrah"

"Hup humpf Hummmph"

"Mmmmmmfooooood!"

77

Chapter Eleven

'Any of that Soup Left?'

All the pirates began to feel warm and the strength began to flow through their bodies. They contentedly licked their lips and patted Belch on the back and it wasn't long before they were all hard at work mending, fixing and patching up the little ship until she was ship-shape and in a seaworthy fashion.

"Ok, crew. All hands on deck, splice the main brace and how about a little bit of 'Wey Hey Heying' the anchor?" The crew rushed to their stations, manning rigging and hoisting sails, and Guff shot up into the crow's nest in order to keep her eyes peeled for land.

The little pirate ship, with her patched up sails and refreshed pirates, slowly began to sail again over the calm seas.

Calmly she sailed, bobbing up and down, up and down.

Belch and Hairy Mole stood side by side at the front of the little ship, keeping an eye on the **horizon**. They had their arms folded and their heads held high as they were both **proud pirates**, having defeated the storm and having helped their friends.

"You know Belch," began Hairy Mole, "if it hadn't have been for that special, salty, green, sea stew of yours we may not have been able to repair this little ship and we may have been lost at sea forever."

"Yep," Belch replied, nodding his head and rocking back and forth on his toes, smiling, proudly.

Hairy Mole raised a hairy eyebrow and continued, "And do you know what Belch . . . it's absolutely amazing how that super soup appeared, when I'm sure that all the cupboards were bare."

79

"Yeeep!" Belch smiled again and shifted his weight, staring into the distance as if he may just have spotted something. "It's a miracle, to be sure," he added.

"Belch?" Hairy Mole turned to his friend "That green, salty, sea soup was whale snot wasn't it?"

Now Hairy Mole looked out to sea while Belch answered him.

"Ask me no questions, Hairy Mole, and I'll tell you no lies."

"Land ahoy, laaaaand ahooooy!!!"

Guff yelled out at the top of her lungs from the crow's nest.

"Hurrah, hurrah," joined in all the pirates.

"Hairy Mole, Hairy Mole." cried the twins, "Land ahoy, we're going home!" The two twins stood in front of their hairy captain with outstretched arms. In front of them they held two bubbling little wooden bowls filled with hot, green, 'soup'. "How about some of Belch's special soup to celebrate?" They looked at Hairy Mole with green 'soup' running down their chins.

"You know lads?" The twins looked at Hairy. "I think I'm going to wait until I get back to Mrs Plop's jam shop."

"More for us then," they whooped and ran to the side of the ship to get a look at the land ahoy.

With that, Hairy Mole put his warty, hairy hand on to Belch's hefty shoulder and looking up at the sunshine above he
smiled

and smiled

and smiled.

BELCH

PICKLE

CREVICE

PIT